Mason
and the
Bees

By
Richard Sinclair

with Illustrations by
Jon Lycett-Smith

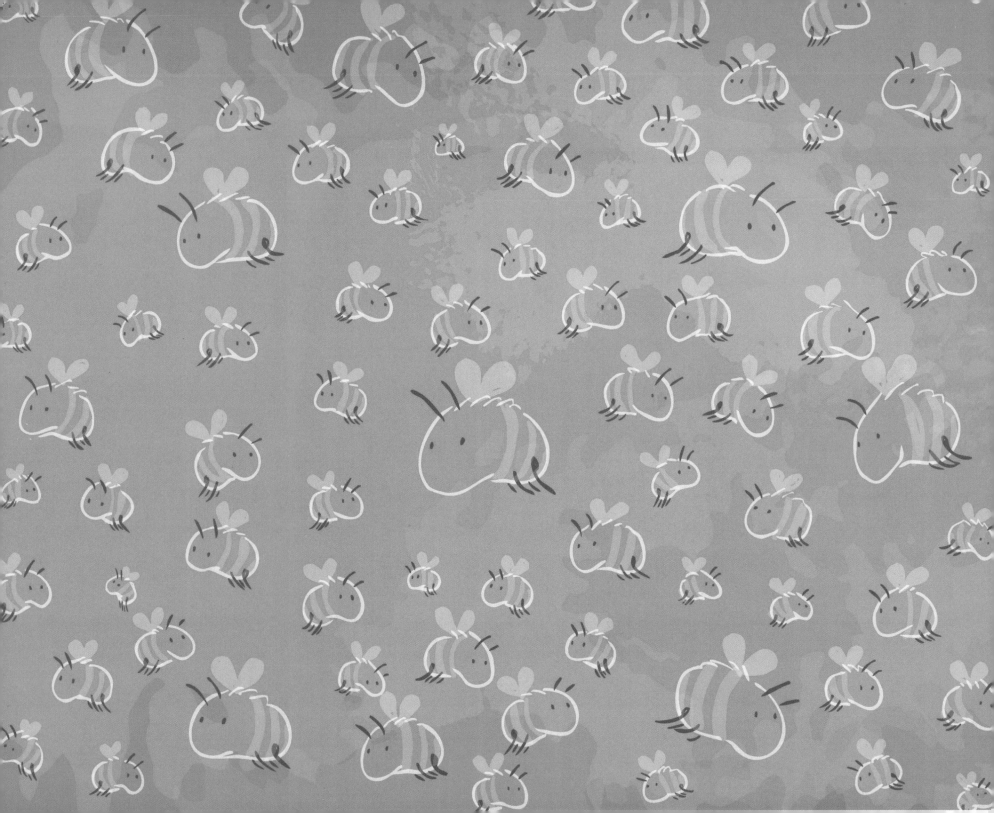

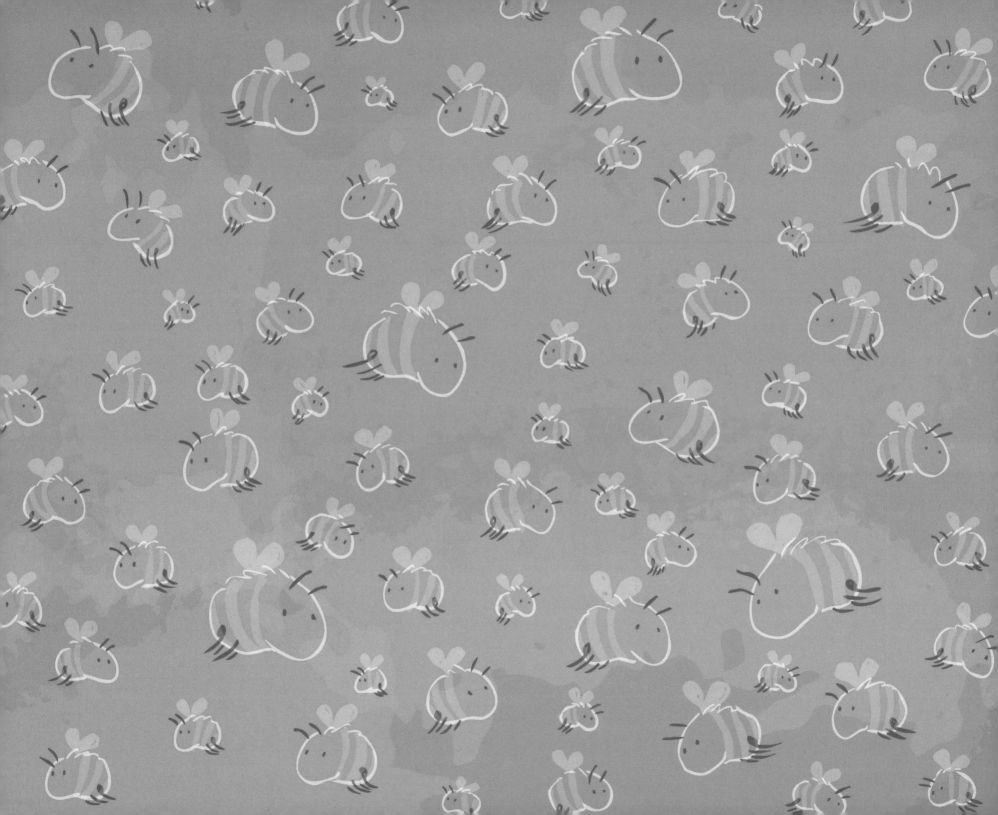

First published 2021
by Rowanvale Books Ltd
The Gate
Keppoch Street
Roath
Cardiff
CF24 3JW
www.rowanvalebooks.com
Library Cataloguing in Publication Data.
A catalogue record for this book is available from the British Library.

RS: For Lewis and Maddi, my constant source of inspiration

JLS: To Charlie, Ivy and Annie, with all my love

Mason was all alone
and locked out in the yard.

His owners had gone out,
so he was left on guard

He was feeling really bored
and wanted food to eat

and he could hear a party
being held just up the street

Mason was a clever dog
and he went to look around
at all the items in the yard
to see what could be found

He noticed things that could be used
to build a grand contraption

and so he set to work
to put his plan in action

Mason knew across the field
there grew a grove of trees

And in those trees, way up high,
there lived a swarm of bees

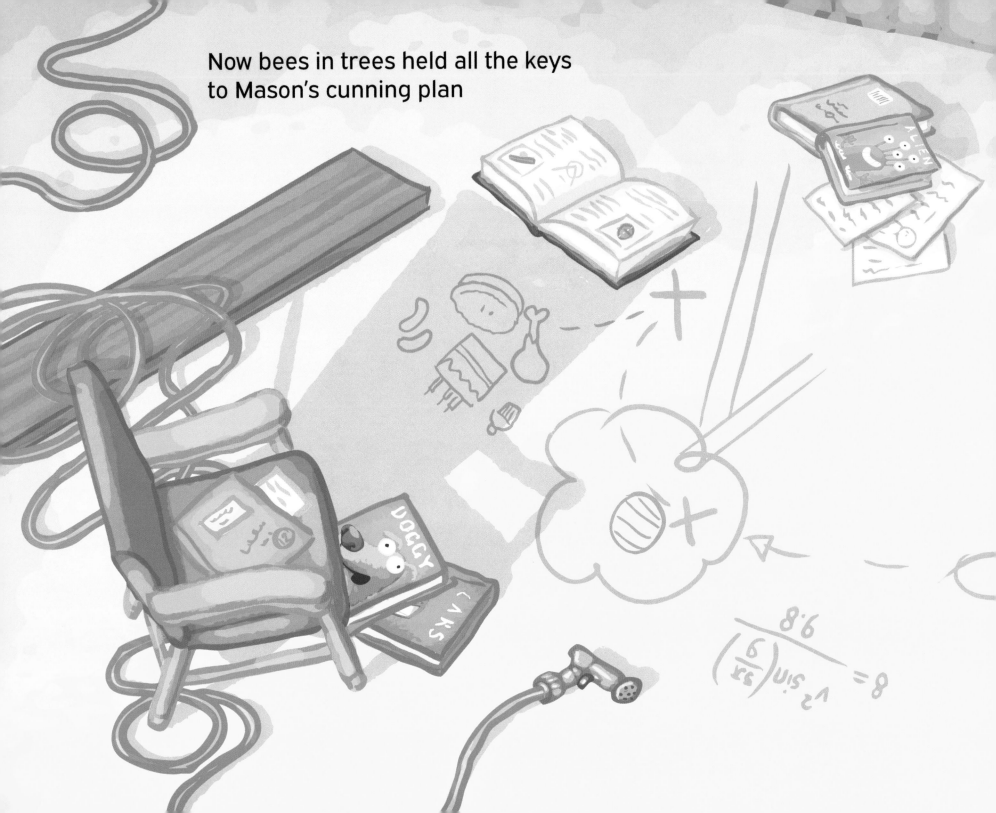

Now bees in trees held all the keys
to Mason's cunning plan

to get the food within his grasp
and so off Mason ran

He balanced books on tables

and he balanced chairs on books

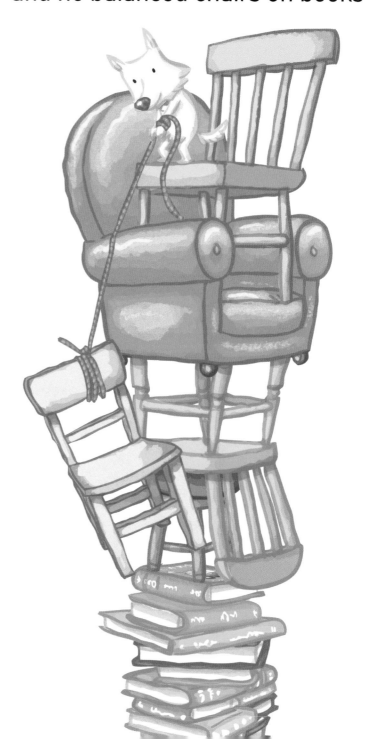

Up and up the tower grew, as unsteady as it looked

Mason climbed up to the very top
Then as quickly as he could

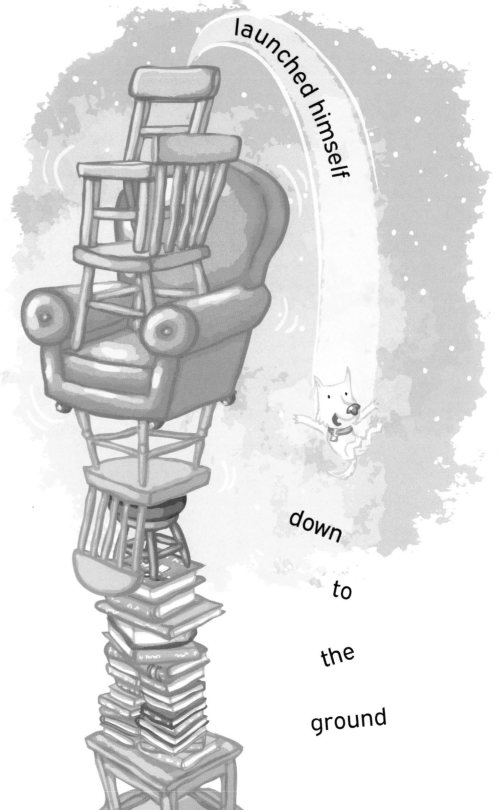

launched himself

down

to

the

ground

onto a plank of wood

He had placed his favourite ball there, one of his many toys

With a whoosh and a woof and a clatter and a bang, he really made a noise

The ball flew through the air
with such amazing speed,

right into the beehive
hanging high up in the trees

It dropped into the party and landed with a crash
Just as the clever dog had planned, it really made a smash

The guests ran from the garden as the bees swarmed all around

Their food and drink forgotten, abandoned on the ground

With the help of a giant fishing rod, the food was finally won
The feast was nearly in his grasp, his plan was almost done

He hooked the steaks, the sausages, the turkey and the pies,
the ham, even the birthday cake—his gastronomic prize

When Mason's owners came back home
they found him fast asleep

With his belly full of party food,
he'd really had a treat

His family had been worried
that Mason would be bored

But Mason just smiled to himself
...and snored and snored and snored...

Mason Phoenix Flame McKay

Author Profile

Richard has been writing books and apps for children since 2013. His stories have been read in over 80 countries and have won numerous awards for creativity and content. He is also a musician and songwriter with his band Murmurs of Earth, an occasional actor, and a dad to two surprisingly well-adjusted children. His stories are based on (semi-) true events.

Website: www.sinclairstories.com
Twitter: @SinclairOnAir

What Did You Think of *Mason and the Bees*?

A big thank you for purchasing this book. It means a lot that you chose this book specifically from such a wide range on offer. I do hope you enjoyed it.

Book reviews are incredibly important for an author. All feedback helps them improve their writing for future projects and for developing this edition. If you are able to spare a few minutes to post a review on Amazon, that would be much appreciated.

Publisher Information

Rowanvale Books provides publishing services to independent authors, writers and poets all over the globe. We deliver a personal, honest and efficient service that allows authors to see their work published, while remaining in control of the process and retaining their creativity. By making publishing services available to authors in a cost-effective and ethical way, we at Rowanvale Books hope to ensure that the local, national and international community benefits from a steady stream of good quality literature.

For more information about us, our authors or our publications, please get in touch.
www.rowanvalebooks.com
info@rowanvalebooks.com

CPSIA information can be obtained at www.ICGtesting.com
Printed in the USA
BVIW121941240321
603354BV00004B/6